Meet My Grandparents

By J. Jean Robertson

Photographs by Jose Luis Pelaez Inc, JenD, Hisele, Pavel Losevsky, Piotr Przeszlo, Maartje van Caspel, Sharon Dominick, Bonnie Jacobs, Luana Mitten, Thomas Mounsey, Yvonne Chamberlain

Frog Street Press, Inc.
www.frogstreet.com

About the Author

J. Jean Robertson graduated from the University of Northern Colorado with a major in home economics and a minor in English. Additional education added to her areas of certification. Jean has taught from pre-school to the college level with some time out for raising her four children. Currently, Jean teaches only as a substitute, freeing her schedule to enjoy her husband, children, and grandchildren.

PHOTO CREDITS: © Jose Luis Pelaez Inc, Getty images: cover; © JenD: page 4; © hisele: page 6; © pavel losevsky: page 8; © Piotr Przeszlo: page 10; © Maartje van Caspel: page 12; © Sharon Dominick: page 14; © Bonnie Jacobs: page 16; © Luana Mitten: page 18; © Thomas Mounsey: page 20; © Yvonne Chamberlain: page 22.

Library of Congress Cataloging-in-Publication Data

Robertson, J. Jean.
  Meet my grandparents / J. Jean Robertson.
    p. cm. -- (The world around me)
  ISBN 978-1-63237-344-1
  Grandparents --Juvenile literature. Grandparent and child --Juvenile literature.

HQ759.9 .R63 2007   2006031491

www.frogstreet.com

Table of Contents

Meeting Grandfathers

My name is Carmina. This is my grandfather. His family came to America from Cuba. I call him Abuelo. We like playing games together.

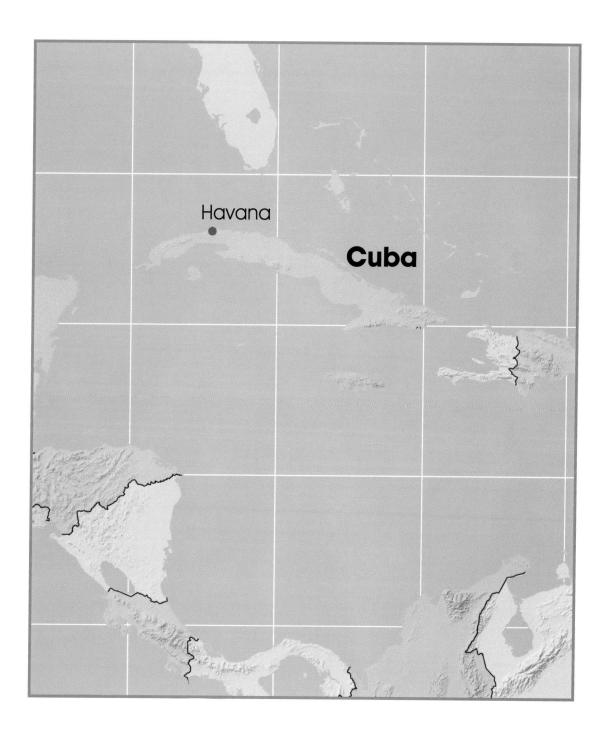

Havana

Cuba

My name is Sammy. This is my grandfather. His family came to America from Jamaica. I call him Poppa. I like it when he visits me and my mom.

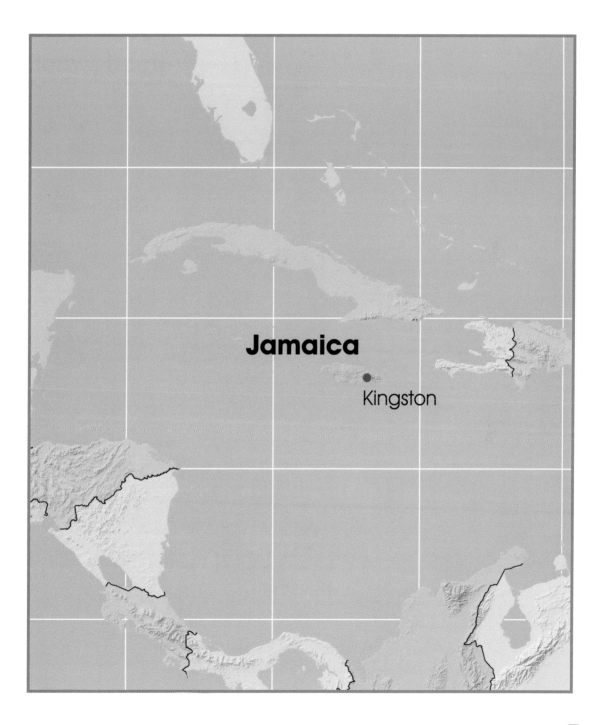

Jamaica

Kingston

My name is Ari. This is my grandfather. His family came to America from Finland. I call him Ukki. I like riding up high on his shoulders.

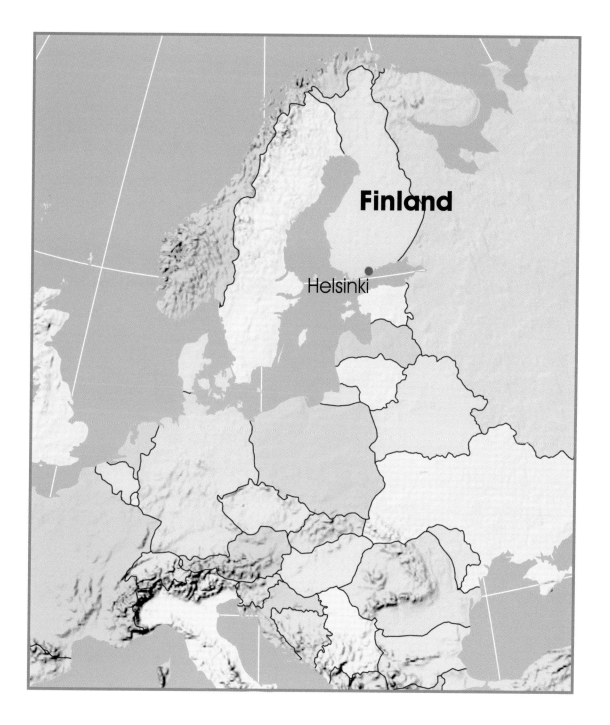

Finland

Helsinki

My name is Tony. This is my grandfather. His family came to America from Italy. I call him Nonno. I like it when he tells me funny stories.

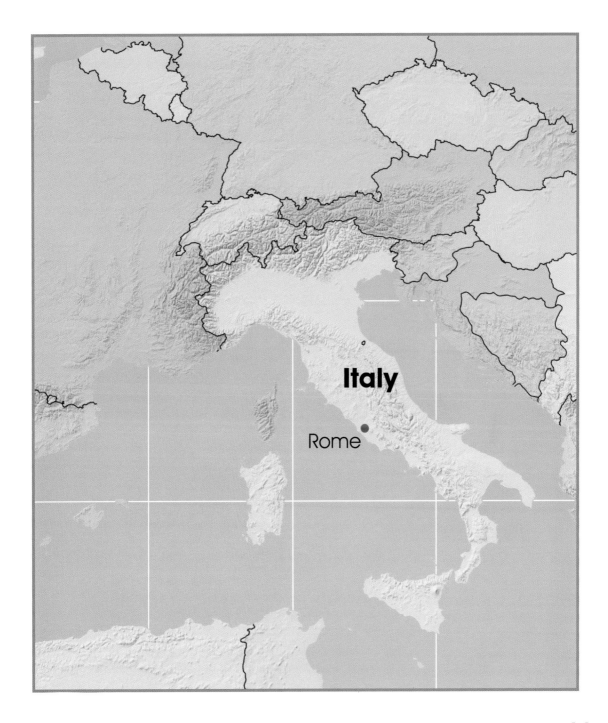

Italy

Rome

My name is Levi. This is my grandfather. His family came to America from Israel. I call him Sabba. We like making snowballs together.

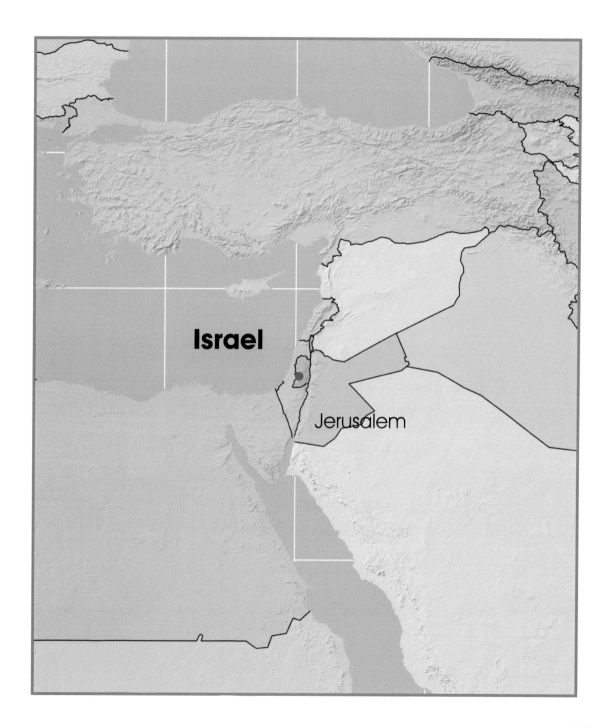

Israel

Jerusalem

Meeting Grandmothers

My name is Blaire. This is my grandmother.
Her family came to America from Scotland.
I call her Grannie. We love sharing secrets.

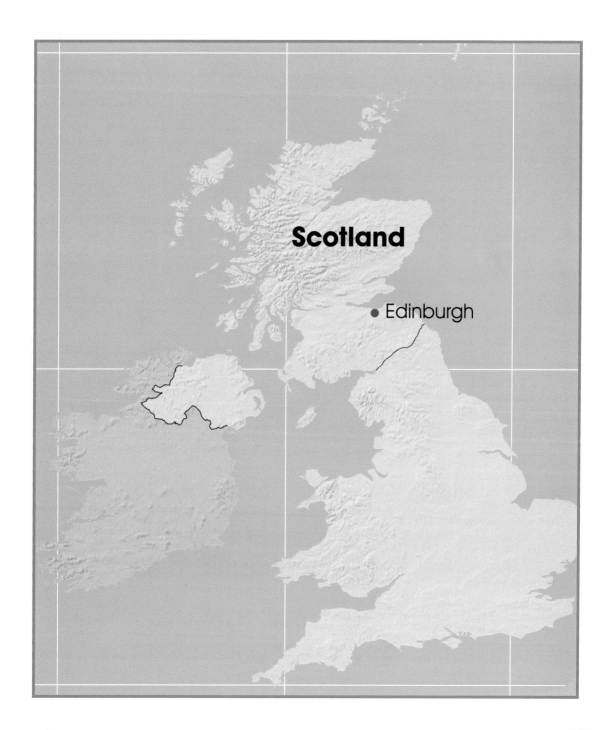

Scotland

● Edinburgh

My name is Tandi. This is my grandmother. Her family came to America from South Africa. My sister, Sezeka, and I call her Mmukulu. We like shopping together.

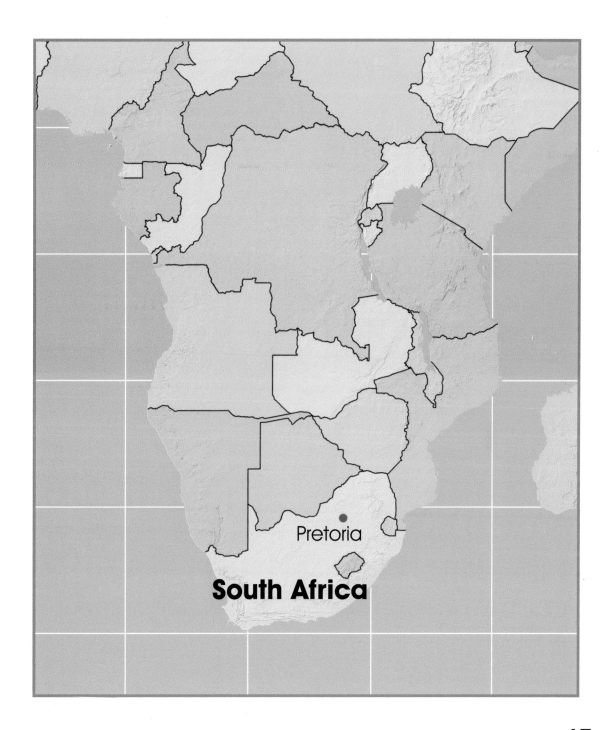

Pretoria

South Africa

My name is Luis. This is my grandmother. Her family came to America from Mexico.
I call her Abuela. We like cooking together.

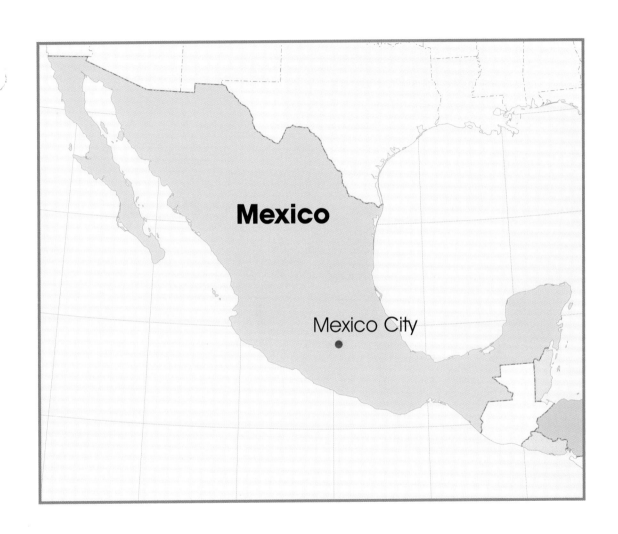

Mexico

Mexico City
•

My name is Michail. This is my grandmother.
Her family came to America from Russia.
I call her Babushka. We like feeding the
birds together.

My name is Hans. This is my grandmother. Her family came to America from The Netherlands. My little brother, Peter, and I call her Oma. We love reading books together!

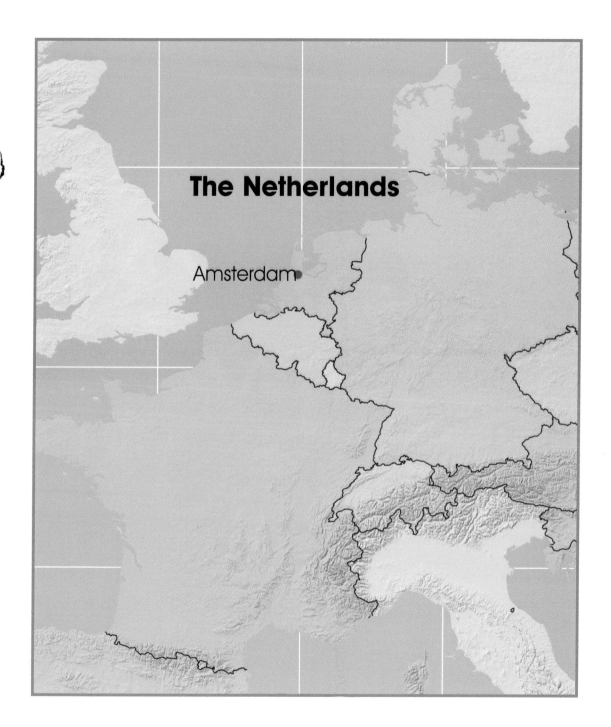

The Netherlands

Amsterdam

Glossary

Abuela (ab WAY la) - Spanish word for grandmother
Nonno (nah NO) - Italian word for grandfather
Oma (o MA) - Dutch word for grandmother

Index